William Twopeny

Extracts From Various Authors

And a letter detailing a fatal banditti adventure in Asia Minor in 1845

William Twopeny

Extracts From Various Authors
And a letter detailing a fatal banditti adventure in Asia Minor in 1845

ISBN/EAN: 9783744752299

Printed in Europe, USA, Canada, Australia, Japan

Cover: Foto ©Andreas Hilbeck / pixelio.de

More available books at **www.hansebooks.com**

EXTRACTS FROM VARIOUS AUTHORS,

AND A LETTER DETAILING A FATAL BANDITTI ADVENTURE IN ASIA MINOR IN 1845.

LONDON:
PRIVATELY PRINTED AT THE
CHISWICK PRESS.
1868.

PREFACE.

HE reason for printing this volume, for private distribution, cannot be better explained, than by the request made in the following letter from the Duchess Dowager of Norfolk.

"Sunday.

"DEAR MR. T.

Last night I was reading some of the Extracts you have bestowed on me, and the occupation brought more vividly than ever, before, a plan of multiplying them by printing, if I can get your leave to do it. It would be a pity to *waste* your time and kindness on a single copy. I would deliver into your hands as many as you chose, if you would give the permission and the name, and advise me how to proceed in doing it.

                    " Most truly obliged,

                              " C. NORFOLK.

" Nov. 22, 1868."

For the arrangement of the contents of this volume, and a few short notes, to which I have put my initials, I alone am answerable.

                    WM. TWOPENY.

48, *Upper Grosvenor Street,*
        December, 1868.

CONTENTS.

Contents.

I.

THE TRANSLATORS OF THE BIBLE TO THE READER.[1]

UT it is high time to shew in briefe what we proposed to ourselves, and what course we helde in this our perusall and survay of the Bible. Truly (good Christian Reader) we never thought from the beginning, that we should need to make a new Translation, nor yet to make of a bad one a good one, (for then the imputation of *Sixtus* had bin

---

[1] Folio. Robert Barker: London, 1613.

When the edition of D'Oyly and Mant's Bible was pub·lished, (4to. Cambridge, 1823,) the address of the Translators to the Reader, an extract from which is here given, was separately printed of the same size, by some Publisher, for those to purchase who desired it. In that impression, the words which in the edition 1613 are "whey instead of milke," are, "wheal instead of milke." Wheal is whey heated scalding hot to take off the curds.—*Richardson's Dict.*—W. T.

true in some sort, that our people had bene fed
with gall of Dragons instead of wine, with whey
instead of milke :) but to make a good one better,
or out of many good ones, one principal good one,
not justly to be excepted against : that hath bene
our endeavour, that our marke. To that purpose
there were many chosen, that were greater in other
mens eyes then in their owne, and that sought the
truth rather then their own praise. Againe, they
came or were thought to come to the worke, not
exercendi causâ (as one saith) but *exercitati*, that is,
learned, not to learne ; for the chiefe overseer and
ἐργοδιώκτης under his Majestie, to whom not only we,
but also our whole Church was much bound, knew
by his wisdome, which thing also *Nazianzen* taught
so long agoe, that it is a preposterous order to teach
first and to learne after, yea that τὸ ἐν πίθῳ κεραμίαν
μανθάνειν, to learne and practise together, is neither
commendable for the workeman nor safe for the
worke.   Therefore such were thought upon, as
could say modestly with Saint *Hierome, Et He-
bræum Sermonem ex parte didicimus, et in Latino
penè ab ipsis incunabulis, &c. detriti sumus. Both we
have learned the Hebrew tongue in part, and in the
Latine we have beene exercised almost from our verie
cradle.* S. *Hierome* maketh no mention of the
Greeke tonge, wherein yet hee did excell, because
hee translated not the olde Testament out of
Greeke, but out of *Hebrew*.   And in what sort did
these assemble ?   In the trust of their owne know-

ledge, or of their sharpenesse of wit, or deepenesse of judgement, as it were an arme of flesh? At no hand. They trusted in him that hath the key of *David*, opening and no man shutting; they prayed to the Lord, the Father of our Lord, to the effect that S. *Augustine* did; *O let thy Scriptures be my pure delight, let me not be deceived in them, neither let me deceive by them.* In this confidence, and with this devotion did they assemble together; not too many, lest one should trouble another, and yet many, lest many things haply might escape them. If you aske what they 'had before them, truely it was the *Hebrew* text of the Olde Testament, the *Greeke* of the New. These are the two golden pipes, or rather conduits, where-through the olive branches emptie themselves into the golde. Saint *Augustine* calleth them precedent, or originall tongues; Saint *Hierome*, fountaines. The same Saint *Hierome* affirmeth, and *Gratian* hath not spared to put it into his Decree, That *as the credit of the olde Bookes* (he meaneth of the Old Testament) *is to bee tryed by the Hebrewe Volumes, so of the Newe by the Greeke tongue,* he meaneth by the originall *Greeke.* If truth be to be tried by these tongues, then whence should a Translation be made, but out of them? These tongues therefore, the Scriptures wee say in those tongues, wee set before us to translate, being the tongues wherein God was pleased to speake to his Church by his Prophets and Apostles. Neither did we run over the worke with that posting haste that the Septuagint did, if that be true which is reported of them, that thay finished it in 72 dayes; neither were we barred or hindered from going over it againe, having once done it, like S. *Hierome*, if that be true which himselfe reporteth, that he could no sooner write anything, but presently it was caught from him, and published, and he could not have leave to mend it ; neither, to be short, were we the first that fell in hand with translating the Scripture into English, and consequently destitute of former helpes, as it is written of *Origen*, that hee was the first in a maner, that put his hand to write commentaries upon the Scriptures, and therefore no marveile, if he overshot himselfe many times. None of these things : the worke hath not bene hudled up in 72 dayes, but hath cost the workemen, as light as it seemeth, the paines of twise seven times seventie-two dayes and more : matters of such weight and consequence are to bee speeded with maturitie : for in a businesse of moment a man feareth not the blame of convenient slacknesse. Neither did wee thinke much[1] to consult the Translators or Commentators, *Chaldee, Hebrewe, Syrian, Greeke or Latine*, no nor the *Spanish, French, Italian,* or *Dutch;* neither did we disdaine to revise that which we had done, and to bring backe to the anvill that which we had hammered: but having

---

[1] *i.e.* "think it much trouble."—W. T.

and using as great helpes as were needfull, and fearing no reproche for slownesse, nor coveting praise for expedition, wee have at the length, through the good hand of the Lord upon us, brought the worke to that passe that you see."

II.

BARROW'S SECOND SERMON, "OF THE DUTY OF
THANKSGIVING."[1]

HEN we contemplate the wonderful works of nature, and, walking about at our leisure, gaze upon the ample theatre of the world, considering the stately beauty, constant order, and sumptuous furniture thereof; the glorious splendour and uniform motion of the heavens; the pleasant fertility of the earth; the curious figure and fragrant sweetness of plants; the exquisite frame of animals; and all other amazing miracles of nature, wherein the glorious attributes of God (especially his transcendent goodness) are most conspicuously displayed; (so that by them not only large acknowledgments, but even gratulatory hymns, as it were, of praise have been extorted from the mouths of

---

[1] "The Sermons of Barrow display a strength of mind, a comprehensiveness and fertility which have rarely been equalled."—*Hallam, Literature of Europe.*—W. T.

Aristotle, Pliny, Galen, and such like men, never suspected guilty of an excessive devotion ;) then should our hearts be affected with thankful sense, and our lips break forth into his praise."

III.

BARROW'S SERMON, "NOT TO OFFEND IN WORD, AN EVIDENCE OF A HIGH PITCH OF VIRTUE."

SPEECH is indeed the rudder that steereth human affairs, the spring that setteth the wheels of action on going; the hands work, the feet walk, all the members and all the senses act by its direction and impulse; yea, most thoughts are begotten, and most affections stirred up thereby: it is itself most of our employment, and what we do beside it, is however guided and moved by it. It is the profession and trade of many, it is the practice of all men, to be in a manner continually talking. The chief and most considerable sort of men manage all their concernments merely by words; by them princes rule their subjects, generals command their armies, senators deliberate and debate about the great matters of state; by them advocates plead causes, and judges decide them; divines perform their offices, and minister their instructions; merchants strike up their bargains, and drive on all their traffick. Whatever almost great or small is done in the court or in the hall, in the church or at the exchange, in the school or in the shop, it is the tongue alone that doeth it : it is the force of this little machine that turneth all the human world about. It is, indeed, the use of this strange organ which rendereth human life, beyond the simple life of other creatures, so exceedingly various and compounded ; which creates such a multiplicity of business, and which transacts it ; while by it we communicate our secret conceptions, transfusing them into others ; while therewith we instruct and advise one another ; while we consult about what is to be done, contest about right, dispute about truth ; while the whole business of conversation, of commerce, of government, and administration of justice, of learning, and of religion, is managed thereby ; yea, while it stoppeth the gap of time, and filleth up the wide intervals of business, our recreations and divertisements (the which do con-stitute a great portion of our life) mainly consisting therein, so that, in comparison thereof, the execu-tion of what we determine and all other action do take up small room : and even all that usually de-pendeth upon foregoing speech, which persuadeth, or counselleth, or commandeth it. Whence the province of speech being so very large, it being so universally concerned, either immediately as the matter, or by consequence as the source of our

actions, he that constantly governeth it well may
justly be esteemed to live very excellently."

After referring, in a later passage, to those who
speak "blasphemously against God, or reproach-
fully concerning religion, or to the disgrace of piety,
with intent to subvert men's faith in God or to
impair their reverence of him," Barrow proceeds:
"This of all impieties is the most prodigiously
gigantic, the most signal practice of enmity towards God, and downright waging of war against
heaven. Of all weapons formed against God, the
tongue most notoriously doth impugn him; for
we cannot reach heaven with our hands, or immediately assault God by our actions: other ill prac-
tices indeed obliquely, or by consequence dishonour
God, and defame goodness; but profane discourse
is directly levelled at them, and doth immediately
touch them, as its formal objects. Now, doing thus
argueth an extremity both of folly and naughtiness; for he that doeth it, either believeth the
existence of God, and the truth of religion; or he
distrusts them. If he doth believe them, what a
desperate madness is it in him, advisedly to invite
certain mischief to his home, and pull down heaviest
vengeance on his own head, by opposing the irre-
sistible power, and invoking the inflexible justice
of God!" After further observations on him who
so acting yet believes, Barrow proceeds to him who
distrusts: "If he cannot believe in God, he may
let them alone who do: if he will not practise reli-

gion, he may forbear to persecute it. He cannot
pretend any zeal; it is therefore only pride that
moves him to disturb us. So may every man with
all the reason in the world complain against the
profane talker. Seeing also it is most evident, that
hearty reverence of God, and a conscientious regard
to religion, do produce great benefits to mankind,
being indeed the main supports of common honesty
and sobriety, the sole curbs, effectually restraining
men from unjust fraud and violence, from brutish
lusts and passions; since apparently religion prescribeth the best rules, and imposeth the strongest
engagements to the performer of those actions,
whereby not only men's private welfare is pro-
moted, and ordinary conversation is sweetened, and
common life is adorned, but also whereby public
order and peace are maintained; since, as Cicero
with good reason judgeth, 'piety being removed, it
is probable that justice itself' (of all virtues the
best guarded and fortified by human power) 'could
not subsist, no faith could be secured, no society
could be preserved among men;' it being mani-
festly vain to fancy, that assuredly without religious
conscience any one will be a good subject, a true
friend, or an honest man; or that any other consideration can induce men to prefer duty to their
prince, the prosperity of their country, fidelity towards their friends or neighbours, before their own
present interests and pleasure; since, I say, the
credit of religion is so very beneficial and useful to

mankind, it is plain that he must be exceedingly
spiteful and malicious, who shall by profane discourse endeavour to supplant or shake it. He that
speaketh against God's providence hath assuredly
a pique at goodness, and would not have it pre-
dominant in the hearts of men. He that disparages
religion doth certainly take his aim against virtue,
and would not have it practised in the world ; his
meaning plainly is, to effect, if he can, that men
should live like beasts in foul impurities, or like
fiends in mischievous iniquities. Such an one
therefore is not to be taken as a simple embracer
of error, but as a spiteful designer against common
good. For, indeed, were any man assured (as none
can upon so much as probable grounds think it)
that religion had been only devised by men, as a
supplemental aid to reason and force, (drawing
them, whom the one could not persuade, nor the
other compel, to the practice of things conducible
to the public weal ;) that it were merely an imple-
ment of policy, or a knack to make people loyal to
their prince, upright in their dealings, sober in their
conversations, moderate in their passions, virtuous
in all their doings ; it were yet a most barbarous
naughtiness and inhumanity in him to assay the
overthrow thereof, with the defeating so excellent
purposes : he that should attempt it, justly would
deserve to be reputed an enemy to the welfare of
mankind, to be treated as a pestilent disturber of
the world."

IV.

BARROW'S SERMON, "A DEFENCE OF THE BLESSED TRINITY."[1]

THAT there is one Divine Nature or Essence, common unto three Persons, incomprehensibly united, and ineffably distinguished; united in essential attributes, distinguished by peculiar idioms and relations; all equally infinite in every perfection, each different from other in order and manner of subsistence; that there is mutual inexistence of one in all, and all in one; a communication without any deprivation or diminution in the communicant; an eternal generation, and an eternal procession, without precedence or succession, without proper causality or dependence; a Father imparting his own, and a Son receiving his Father's life, and a Spirit issuing from both, without any division or multiplication of essence; these are notions which

---

[1] "The Trinity," says South, "is a fundamental article of the Christian religion; and as he that denies it may lose his soul, so he that too much strives to understand it, may lose his wits."—W. T.

may well puzzle our reason in conceiving how they agree, but should not stagger our faith in assenting that they are true ; upon which we should meditate, not with hope to comprehend, but with disposition to admire, veiling our faces in the presence, and prostrating our reason at the feet of wisdom so far transcending us."

V.

BARROW'S SERMON, "OF FAITH."

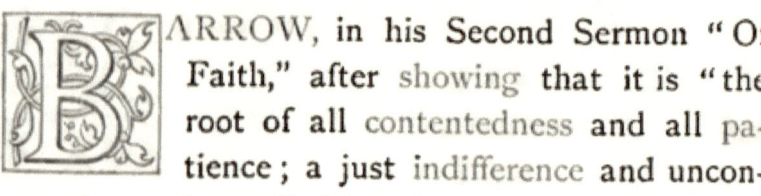ARROW, in his Second Sermon "Of Faith," after showing that it is "the root of all contentedness and all patience; a just indifference and unconcernedness about all things here; that it alone can untack our minds and affections from this world, rearing our souls from earth and fixing them in heaven," &c. &c. proceeds thus: "But you will perhaps interpose and say: These are indeed fine sayings, but where do such effects appear? Who, I pray, doth practise according to these notions? Where is that gallant to be found, who doth work so great exploits? Where may we discern that height of piety, that tenderness of charity, that meek comportment with injuries and affronts, that clear sincerity, that depth of humility, that strictness of temperance, that perfect contentedness and undisturbed calmness of mind, that stoutness of courage and stiffness of patience, which you talk of as the undoubted issues of faith? Who is the man that with such glee doth hug afflictions, or

biddeth adversity so welcome to his home? Where
dwell they, who so little regard this world, or so
much affect the other? Do we not see men run as
if they were wild after preferment, wealth, and
pleasure? What do they else, but scrape and
scramble and scuffle for these things? Doth not
every man moan the scantness of his lot, doth not
every man flinch at any trouble, doth not every
one with all his might strive to rid himself of any
thing disgustful to his sense or fancy? Are not,
therefore, such encomiums of faith mere specula-
tions, or brave rhodomontades of divinity? The
objection, I confess, is a shrewd one; but I must
reply to it: You say, where are such effects, where
are such men? I ask then, Where is faith, where
are believers? Shew me the one, and I will shew
you the other: if such effects do not appear, it is
no argument that faith cannot produce them, but a
sign that faith is wanting; as if a tree doth not put
forth in due season, we conclude the root is dead;
if a fountain yield no streams, we suppose it dried
up. *Shew me*, saith St. James, *thy faith by thy
works;* implying, that if good works do not shine
forth in the conversation, it is suspicious there is no
true faith in the heart; for such faith is not a feeble
weening, or a notion swimming in the head, it is
not a profession issuing from the mouth, it is not
following such a garb, or adhering to such a party,
but a persuasion fixed in the heart, by firm resolution, by lively sense; *it is with the heart*, as St.

Paul saith, *man believeth unto righteousness;* that
is the faith we speak of, and to which we ascribe
the production of so great and worthy effects ; if
a man wanteth that, attested by practice suitable,
though he know all the points exactly, though he
will readily say *Amen* to every article of the Creed,
though he wear all the badges of a Christian,
though he frequent the congregations, and comply
with the forms of our religion, yet is he really an
infidel ; for is he not an infidel who denieth God ?
and is he not such a renegado who liveth impiously ?
he is so in St. Paul's account ; for, *They profess,*
saith he of such persons, *that they know God, but in
works they deny Him :* and, *He is not a Jew,* saith
the same apostle, (he is not a Christian, may we by
parity of reason affirm,) *who is one outwardly; but
he is a Christian who is one inwardly, and faith is
that of the heart, in the spirit, and not in the letter,
whose praise is not of man, but of God:* we may
attribute to a barren conceit, or to a formal profession, the name of faith, but it is in an equivocal
or wide sense ; as a dead man is called a man, or a
dry stick resting in the earth a tree ; for so *faith,*
saith St. James, *without works is dead;* is, indeed,
but a trunk, or carcase of faith, resembling it in
outward shape, but void of its *spirit* and life."

D

VI.

BARROW'S SERMON, "THE BEING OF GOD PROVED FROM THE FRAME OF HUMAN NATURE."

N Barrow's Sermon, "The Being of God proved from the Frame of Human Nature," after describing several "fair characters of the Divine nature engraven upon man's soul," he proceeds: "But one chief property thereof we have not as yet touched; whereof, alas! the lineaments are more faint and less discernible; they being in themselves originally most tender and delicate, and thence apt, by our unhappy degeneration, to suffer the most, and have thence accordingly been most defaced; goodness I mean; whereof yet, I shall not doubt to say, many goodly relics are extant, and may be observed therein. There do remain, dispersed in the soil of human nature, divers seeds of goodness, of benignity, of ingenuity, which being cherished, excited, and quickened by good culture, do, to common experience, thrust out flowers very lovely, yield fruits very pleasant of virtue and goodness. We see that even the generality of men are prone

to approve the laws and rules directing to justice, sincerity, and beneficence ; to commend actions suitable unto them, to honour persons practising according to them ; as also to distaste, detest, or despise such men, whose principles or tempers incline them to the practice of injury, fraud, malice, and cruelty ; yea, even them men generally are apt to dislike, who are so addicted to themselves as to be backward to do good to others. Yea, no man can act according to those rules of justice and goodness, without satisfaction of mind ; no man can do against them without inward self-condemnation and regret (as St. Paul did observe for us). No man hardly is so savage, in whom the receiving kindnesses doth not beget a kindly sense, and an inclination (*eo nomine*, for that cause barely) to return the like ; which inclination cannot well be ascribed to any other principle than somewhat of ingenuity innate to man. All men, I suppose, feel in themselves (if at least not hardened by villanous custom) a disposition prompting them to commiserate, yea (even with some trouble and some damage to themselves) to succour and relieve them who are in want, pain, or any distress ; even mere strangers, and such from whom they can expect no return of benefit or advantage to themselves."

VII.

BARROW'S SERMON, "THE BEING OF GOD PROVED FROM SUPERNATURAL EFFECTS."

HEY are much mistaken, who place a kind of wisdom in being very incredulous, and unwilling to assent to any testimony, how full and clear soever; for this indeed is not wisdom, but the worst kind of folly. It is folly, because it causes ignorance and mistake, with all the consequents of these; and it is very bad, as being accompanied with disingenuity, obstinacy, rudeness, uncharitableness, and the like bad dispositions; from which credulity itself, the other extreme sort of folly is exempt. Compare we, I say, these two sorts of fools; the credulous fool, who yields his assent hastily upon any slight ground; and the suspicious fool, who never will be stirred by any the strongest reason or clearest testimony; we shall find the latter in most respects the worst of the two; that his folly arises from worse causes, hath worse adjuncts, produceth worse effects. Credulity may spring from an airy

complexion, **or from a** modest opinion **of** one's self ; suspiciousness hath its birth from an earthy temper of body, or from self-conceit in the mind ; *that* carries with it being civil **and** affable, and **apt to** correct an **error** ; with *this* **a man** is intractable, unwilling to hear, stiff and incorrigible in his ignorance or mistake ; *that* begets speed **and** alacrity in action ; *this* renders **a man** heavy and dumpish, slow and tedious in his resolutions and in his proceedings : *both* include want of judgment ; **but** *this* pretending to more thereof, becomes thereby **more** dangerous. Forward rashness, which is the same with *that,* **may** sometimes, like an acute disease, undo a man sooner ; **but** stupid dotage, little differing from *this,* is (like a chronical distemper) commonly more mischievous, and always more hard **to** cure. **In fine, were men** in their other affairs, **or in** ordinary converse, so diffident to plain testimony, as some do seem to be in these matters concerning religion, they would soon feel great inconveniences to proceed thence ; their business would stick, their conversation would be distasteful ; they would be much more offensive, and no less ridiculous than the most credulous fool in the world. While men therefore so perversely distrustful affect to seem wise, **they** affect really to **be** fools ; **and** practise according to the worst **sort of** folly."

VIII.

BARROW'S SERMON, "MAKER OF HEAVEN AND EARTH."

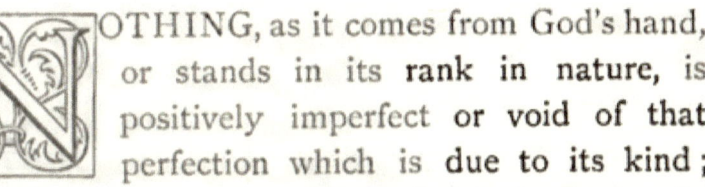OTHING, as it comes from God's hand, or stands in its rank in nature, is positively imperfect or void of that perfection which is due to its kind; much less is any creature absolutely bad, that is, ugly, or noxious, or troublesome, or cumbersome to the universe; so that it were better away out of it, than in it. *God*, saith the Hebrew wise man, *created all things, that they might have their being, and the generations of the world were healthful, and there is no poison of destruction in them.* Everything contributes somewhat to the use and benefit, or to the beauty and ornament of the whole: no weed grows out of the earth, no insect creeps upon the ground, which hath not its elegancy, and yields not its profit; nothing is abominable or despicable, though all things are not alike amiable and admirable : there is therefore nothing in all the compass of nature unfit or unworthy to have proceeded

from God ; nothing which he beseemingly, without
derogation to his excellencies, may not own for his
work ; nothing which in its rank and degree doth
not confer to the manifestation of **his** glorious
power, admirable wisdom, and excellent goodness :
O Lord, (cried the devout Psalmist upon particular
survey and consideration of them,) *how manifold
are thy works ! in wisdom hast thou made them all;
the earth is full of thy riches.* That which **we call**
poison, **is such** only relatively, **being noxious or
destructive to one part, but** innocent, **wholesome,
and** useful **to** some other part ; and never prejudicial to the whole body of things ; yea, even to
that part itself **it is commonly** beneficial in some
case or season ; affording, if not continual alimony,
yet sometime physic thereto, and serving to expel
another poison or mischief **more** imminently dangerous.   That which we call a monster, **is not** un-
natural in regard to the whole contexture of causes,
but ariseth **no** less methodically, **than** anything
most ordinary ; **and it** also hath its good end and
use, well serving **to** illustrate the beauty and con-
venience of nature's usual course. As for pain and
grief incident to the nature of things, without regard
to any demerit or justice, they are **not** properly
evils, but adherences to the less perfect natures of
things ; **in a** state liable to which God not **only**
justly, but wisely, according to his pleasure, might
constitute things, for the reasons and ends **before**
insinuated ; **for no** reason **obliged** him **to confer**

upon everything extreme perfection ; he might dis-
pense his liberalities in what kind and measure he
thought good.   In fine, the reason of offence we
take at anything of this kind, seeming bad or
ugly to us, ariseth from our defect of knowledge
and sagacity, we not being able to discern the
particular tendency of each thing to the common
utility and benefit of the world."

IX.

BARROW'S SERMON, "OF THE EXCELLENCY OF
THE CHRISTIAN RELIGION."

T is a peculiar excellency of our religion,
that it prescribeth an accurate rule of
life, most congruous to reason, and suitable to our nature; most conducible to
our welfare and our content; most apt to procure
each man's private good, and to promote the public
benefit of all; by the strict observance whereof we
shall do what is worthy of ourselves and most becoming us; yea, shall advance our nature above
itself into a resemblance of the Divine nature; we
shall do God right, and obtain his favour; we shall
oblige and benefit men, acquiring withal good-will
and good respect from them; we shall purchase to
ourselves all the conveniences of a sober life, and
all the comforts of a good conscience. For, if we
first examine the precepts directive of our practice
in relation to God, what can be more just, or
comely, or pleasant, or beneficial to us, than are
those duties of piety, which our religion doth en-
join? What can be more fit, than that we should

E

most highly esteem and honour him, who is most
excellent ? That we should bear most hearty affec-
tion to him, who is in himself most good, and most
beneficial to us ? That we should have a most
awful dread of him, who is so infinitely powerful,
holy, and just ? That we should be very grateful
unto him from whom we have received our being,
with all the comforts and conveniences thereof ?
That we should entirely trust and hope in him,
who can do what he will, and will do whatever in
reason we can expect from his goodness, and can
never fail to perform what he hath promised ?
That we should render all obedience and observance to him, whose children, whose servants, whose
subjects we are born ; by whose protection and
provision we enjoy our life and livelihood ? Can
there be a higher privilege than liberty of access,
with assurance of being favourably received in our
needs, to him, who is thoroughly able to supply
them ? Can we desire upon easier terms to receive benefits, than by acknowledging our wants,
and asking for them ? Can there be required a
more gentle satisfaction from us for our offences,
than confession of them, accompanied with repentance and effectual resolution to amend ? Is it not,
in fine, most equal and fair, that we should be
obliged to promote his glory, who hath obliged
himself to furnish our good ? The practice of such
a piety, as it is apparently a reasonable service,
so it cannot but produce excellent fruits of ad-

vantage to ourselves, a joyful peace of conscience, and a comfortable hope, a freedom from all superstitious terrors and scruples, from all tormenting cares and anxieties : it cannot but draw down from God's bountiful hands showers of blessings upon our heads, and of joys into our hearts ; whence our obligation to these duties is not only reasonable, but very desirable."

After showing the state into which man when unaided falls, the author proceeds : " From this unhappy plight our religion thoroughly doth rescue us, assuring us, that God Almighty is not only reconcilable, but desirous, upon good terms, to become our friend, himself most frankly proposing overtures of grace, and soliciting us to close with them ; it upon our compliance tendereth, under God's own hand and seal, a full discharge of all guilts and debts, however contracted ; it receiveth a man into perfect favour and friendship, if he doth not himself wilfully reject them, or resolve to continue at distance, in estrangement and enmity toward God. It proclaimeth, that if we be careful to amend, God will not be extreme to mark what we do amiss ; that iniquity, if we do not incorrigibly affect and cherish it, shall not be our ruin ; that although by our infirmity, we fall often, yet by our repentance we may rise again, and by our sincerity shall stand upright ; that our endeavours to serve and please God (although imperfect and defective, if serious and sincere) will be accepted by him.

This is the tenor of that great covenant between
heaven and earth, which the Son of God did procure by his intercession, did purchase by his merits
of wonderful obedience and patience, did ratify and
seal by his blood ; did publish to mankind, did
confirm by miraculous works, did solemnize by
holy institutions, doth by the evangelical ministry
continually recommend to all men ; so that we can
nowise doubt of its full accomplishment on God's
part, if we be not deficient in ours : so to our ines-
timable benefit and unspeakable comfort doth our
religion ease their conscience, and encourage them
in the practice of their duty, who do sincerely em-
brace it, and firmly adhere thereto. The last advantage which I shall mention of this doctrine is
this : that it propoundeth and asserteth itself in a
manner very convincing and satisfactory : it propoundeth itself in a style and garb of speech, as
accommodate to the general capacity of its hearers,
so proper to the authority which it claimeth, becoming the majesty and sincerity of divine truth ;
it expresseth itself plainly and simply, without any
affectation or artifice, without ostentation of wit or
eloquence, such as men study to insinuate and im-
press their devices by : it also speaketh with an
imperious and awful confidence, such as argueth
the speaker satisfied both of his own wisdom and
authority ; that he doubteth not of what he saith
himself, that he knoweth his hearers obliged to believe him ; its words are not like the words of a wise

man, who is wary and careful **that he** slip not into mistake, (interposing therefore now and then his may be's and perchances,) nor like the words of a learned scribe, grounded **on** semblances **of** reason, and backed with testimonies ; nor **as** the words **of** a crafty sophister, who by long circuits, subtile fetches, and sly trains of discourse doth inveigle men **to** his opinion ; **but, like** the words **of a king,** carrying with them authority and power uncontrollable, commanding forthwith attention, assent, and obedience ; this you are to believe, **this you are** to do, upon pain of our high displeasure, at your utmost peril be it ; your life, your salvation de-pendeth thereon ; such **is the** style **and tenor** thereof, plainly such as becometh the sovereign Lord **of** all to use, when he shall please **to pro-**claim his mind and will unto us."

X.

BARROW'S SERMON, "THE REASONABLENESS AND
EQUITY OF A FUTURE JUDGMENT.

FROM God's permitting good men to suffer, how smartly soever, nothing can be inferred prejudicial unto divine goodness or justice; since they are thereby made fitter for, and do attain a surer title to, those excellent rewards, which he upon such trial and approbation of their virtues doth intend to confer upon them; especially considering that afflictions are necessary, both as means of rendering men good, and as occasions of expressing their goodness, that scarce any virtue could subsist or could appear without them. There could be no such thing as patience, if there were no adversities to be endured; no such thing as contentedness, if there were no wants to be felt; no such thing as industry, if there were to be no pains to be taken; no such thing as humility, if sensible infirmities and crosses did not prompt us to sober thoughts, and show us what we are. There would be no true wisdom, no clear knowledge of ourselves, or right judgment of things, without experiencing the worst half of things. We should never learn to master our passions, or temper our appetites, or wrest our inclinations to a compliance with reason, if that discipline were away, which the holy Psalmist intimateth, saying : *It is good for me that I have been afflicted, that I might learn Thy statutes.* How much we do love God, how submissive we are to God's will, how little we do value these mean things here, we cannot otherwise than by willingly undergoing or patiently bearing afflictions, well express ; without it no sure trial of virtue can be, without it no excellent example of goodness had ever been. As, therefore, it is necessary that good men, even that they may be good, should suffer here ; so it is, supposing a future judgment, very just that they should do so, that they may acquire a title to the rewards following it ; rewards far outweighing the light afflictions they are put to endure here."

Further on the author proceeds thus : " This life is not a time of reaping, but of sowing ; not of approbation, but of trial ; not of triumph, but of combat : this world is not a place of enjoyment, but of work ; our condition here is not a state of settlement, but of travel ; whence no man should expect more of encouragement than is needful to support him in this work and way ; should look to receive wages before his task is done ; to get the prize, before he hath gone through the race ; to

gather the spoils before he hath fought out the
battle ; to enjoy rest, before he is at his journey's
end ; to be put in full possession of happiness, before his right and title thereto is completely assured :
no man also should presume or please himself upon
present impunity for his misbehaviour or sloth, like
those of whom the Preacher saith : *Because sentence
against an evil work is not executed speedily, therefore
the heart of the sons of men is fully set in them to do
evil ;* seeing this is the season of mercy and patience,
when God commonly doth not further inflict crosses
on us than may serve to mind us of our duty, or
urge us to the performance of it ; and seeing the
longer vengeance is withheld, the more heavy it will
at last fall on us, if we despise the present season of
grace, and proceed to the end in impenitence ; present impunity, therefore, is a sore punishment, and
correction here a really great favour."

XI.

SWIFT'S SERMON ON SLEEPING IN CHURCH.

" And there sat in the window a certain young man, named Eutychus, being fallen into a deep sleep; and while Paul was long preaching, he sunk down with sleep, and fell down from the third loft, and was taken up dead."—Acts xx. 9.

 HAVE chosen these words with design, if possible, to disturb some part of this audience of half an hour's sleep, for the convenience and exercise whereof, this place, at this season of the day, is very much celebrated.

"There is, indeed, one mortal disadvantage to which all preaching is subject ; that those who, by the wickedness of their lives, stand in greatest need, have usually the smallest share ; for either they are absent upon the account of idleness, or spleen, or hatred to religion, or in order to doze away the intemperance of the week : or, if they do come, they are sure to employ their minds rather any other way, than regarding or attending to the business of the place.

" The accident which happened to this young man in the text, hath not been sufficient to discourage his successors ; but, because the preachers now in the world, however they may exceed St. Paul in the art of setting men to sleep, do extremely fall short of him in the working of miracles ; therefore men are become so cautious as to choose more safe and convenient stations and postures for taking their repose, without hazard of their persons ; and, upon the whole matter, choose rather to trust their destruction to a miracle, than their safety." [1]

---

[1] To this Sermon, Sir Walter Scott, in his edition of Swift's Works, has the following note :—

" If the following discourse did not prove a lasting and effectual cure of the malady referred to in the Dean's congregation, it must be allowed at least to have possessed the merit of a temporary remedy ; since it is hardly possible to conceive that any one should indulge in slumber during the delivery."   W. T.

XII.

DR. JOHNSON'S LIFE OF SIR THOMAS BROWNE.

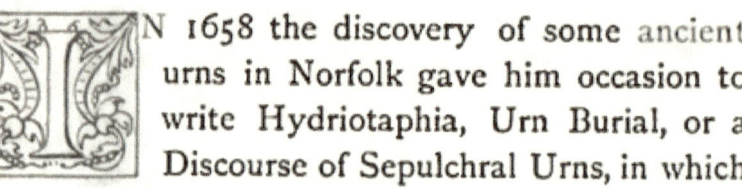N 1658 the discovery of some ancient urns in Norfolk gave him occasion to write Hydriotaphia, Urn Burial, or a Discourse of Sepulchral Urns, in which he treats with his usual learning on the funeral rites of the ancient nations; exhibits their various treatment of the dead; and examines the substances found in his Norfolcian urns. There is, perhaps, none of his works which better exemplifies his reading or memory. It is scarcely to be imagined how many particulars he has amassed together, in a treatise which seems to have been occasionally written; and for which, therefore, no materials could have been previously collected. It is, indeed, like other treatises of antiquity, rather for curiosity than use; for it is of small importance to know which nation buried their dead in the ground, which threw them into the sea, or which gave them to birds and beasts; when the practice of cremation began, or when it was disused; whether the bones of different

persons were mingled in the same urn ; what obla-
tions were thrown into the pyre ; or how the ashes
of the body were distinguished from those of other
substances.   Of the uselessness of all these enquiries, Browne seems not to have been ignorant ; and
therefore concludes them with an observation which
can never be too frequently recollected.

"'All or most apprehensions rested in opinions
of some future being, which ignorantly or coldly
believed, begat those perverted conceptions, cere-
monies, sayings, which Christians pity or laugh at.
Happy are they, which live not in that disadvantage
of time, when men could say little for futurity, but
from reason ; whereby the noblest minds fell often
upon doubtful deaths and melancholy dissolutions :
with these hopes Socrates warmed his doubtful
spirits, against the cold potion ; and Cato, before
he durst give the fatal stroke, spent part of the
night in reading the immortality of Plato, thereby
confirming his wavering hand unto the animosity of
that attempt.

"'It is the heaviest stone that melancholy can
throw at man, to tell him that he is at the end of
his nature ; or that there is no further state to
come, unto which this seems progressional, and
otherwise made in vain : without this accomplishment, the natural expectation and desire of such a
state were but a fallacy in nature ; unsatisfied con-
siderators would quarrel the justice of their consti-
tution, and rest content that Adam had fallen

lower, whereby, by knowing no other original, **and** deeper ignorance of themselves, **they** might have enjoyed the happiness of inferior creatures, who **in** tranquillity possess these constitutions, **as** having not the apprehension to deplore their own natures ; and being framed below the circumference **of** these hopes **or** cognition of better things, **the wisdom of** God hath necessitated their contentment. But **the** superior ingredient and **obscured** part of ourselves, whereto all present **felicities afford no** resting **con-**tentment, will be able at **last** to tell us we are more than our present selves : and evacuate such hopes **in** the fruition of their own accomplishments.'"

XIII.

SIR THOMAS BROWNE ON DREAMS.[1]

HALF our days we pass in the shadow of the earth; and the brother of death exacteth a third part of our lives. A good part of our sleep is peered out with visions and fantastical objects, wherein we are confessedly deceived. The day supplieth us with truths, the night with fictions and falsehoods, which uncomfortably divide the natural account of our beings. And, therefore, having passed the day in sober labours and rational enquiries of truth, we are fain to betake ourselves unto such a state of being, wherein the soberest heads have acted all the monstrosities of melancholy, and which unto open eyes are no better than folly and madness."

---

[1] The observations of Sir Thomas Browne on Dreams, of which the opening paragraph only is here given, were first published in the fourth volume of the 8vo. edition of his works, 1835.—W. T.

XIV.

JOURNAL OF EDWARD BROWNE, SON OF SIR THOMAS BROWNE.

ANUARY 1 (1663-64). I was at Mr. Howard's,[1] brother to the Duke of Norfolk, who kept his Christmas this year at the Duke's Palace in Norwich, so magnificently as the like hath scarce been seen. They had dancing every night, and gave entertainments to all that would come ; hee built up a roome, on purpose to dance in, very large, and hung with the bravest hangings I ever saw ; his candlesticks, snuffers, tongues, fire-shovels and andirons, were silver ; a banquet was given every night after dancing ; and three coaches were employed to fetch ladies every afternoon, the greatest of which would holde fourteen persons, and coste five hundred pound, without the harnesse, which coste six score more."

---

[1] The Mr. Howard here mentioned was afterwards sixth Duke of Norfolk.—W. T.

XV.

The following extracts are given, one from Henderson's "Journal of a Residence in Iceland," 2nd edition, 1819, the other from Bishop Heber's "Hymns," on account of the coincidence of thought between two minds, each deeply imbued with grateful piety.—W. T.

ENDERSON, after describing a magnificent scene, says (p. 190) :—" How vast and glorious are the works of God! How they reflect the splendour, majesty, and unlimited perfection of their Maker! But if such be the grandeur and beauty of creation ; if the eye be dazzled with its lustre, and the most capacious mind be unable to grasp its immensity, how infinitely more excellent and glorious must HE be, to whose all creative word they owe their excellence, who dwells in light inaccessible ; and before whom *' the nations are as a drop of a bucket, and are counted as the small dust of the balance.'* "

> " I praised the earth in beauty seen,
> With garlands gay of various green,
> I praised the sea, whose ample field
> Shone glorious like a silver shield,

And earth and ocean seem'd to say,
'Our beauties are but for a day.'

I praised the sun, whose chariot roll'd
On wheels of amber and of gold,
I praised the moon, whose softer eye
Gleam'd sweetly through the summer sky,
And moon and sun in answer said,
'Our days of light are numbered.'

O God! O good beyond compare!
If thus Thy meaner works are fair,
If thus Thy beauties gild the span
Of ruin'd earth and sinful man,
How glorious must the mansion be
Where Thy redeemed dwell with Thee.'

XVI.

END OF BOTHWELL'S CAREER.[1]

AN item remains in the winding up of the tragic story, before we open a new chapter in history. The remorseless villain of the plot, who has bent a finer nature than his own to his evil purposes, has to be disposed of. It is an end quickly told. He escaped to his dukedom of Orkney—that one of his feudal estates which was farthest off from the avenging power. It was long believed that in his island principality he got a small fleet fitted out, with which he turned pirate captain in the north seas. This was a suitable end for such a career, according to the rules of the romances ; but to a man so marked and pursued, for whom every sea would be swept, the attempt would be certain destruction. Grange was in pursuit of him, and in dire emergency he made vehement efforts to get the means of escape to the northern states of the Continent. It hap-

---

[1] Burton's " History of Scotland," vol. iv. pp. 454-57.

pened that he thus purchased the vessel of a troublesome pirate named David Wodt. When this craft
was seen off the Danish coast, it was naturally under suspicion ; and when it was taken in charge by a
Danish ship, and Bothwell found in command, and
in the broken-down condition of one fleeing from
justice, there naturally followed an investigation
when he was landed at Bergen. His story, that he
was a king in difficulties, made the affair inexpli-
cable and wonderful ; but it was soon seen that he
was not the pirate who had transacted business in
the ship he sailed in.[1]

" He seems to have become popular—to have been
getting, as it were, into society—in this northern
region, when trouble came upon him in a shape
that, affecting the final destiny of a life like his, has,
by contrast, an air of the ludicrous. He was claimed

---

[1] We owe these revelations to a justly popular writer of
travels in Northern Europe, who, finding himself in the scenes
of Bothwell's latter days, thought it worth while discovering
what local records there were of his sojourn. He found in the
record which he terms the Liber Bergensis, how, "September 2, A.D. 1568, came the king's ship David, upon which
Christian of Aalborg was head man. He had taken prisoner
a count from Scotland of the name of Jacob Hebroe of
Botwile, who first was made Duke of the Orkneys and Shet-
land, and lately married the Queen of Scotland, and after he
was suspected of having been in the counsel to blow up the
king. They first accused the Queen, and then the Count, but
he made his escape and came to Norway ; and was afterwards taken to Denmark by the king's ship David."

Marryat's Jutland, chap. xxvii.

by a certain Anna, daughter of Christopher Trandson, as her husband, who had deserted her ; and it
seems to have been on this charge, and not for any
reason of state, that he was detained in the Castle
of Malmoe.[1]

"Strong demands were made for his extradition
both by England and Scotland, but they were re-
sisted.   The Danish Government offered to put him
on trial, under their own laws, and before their own
courts, for any crime he might be charged with, but
would not give him up.

"There was a rumour that he had died in 1573.
It was received as conclusive in England and Scotland, and the name of Bothwell belonged only to
the past.   It would seem, however, that this rumour
was propagated to save Denmark from the pursuit
of the troublesome pressure to render him up.   Bothwell, at all events, lived down to the year 1577,

---

[1] On the 17th of September "Mrs. Anna, Christopher
Trandson's daughter, brought a suit against the Earl of
Bothwell, for having taken her away from her native country,
and refusing to treat her as his married wife, although he by
hand, word of mouth, and by letters had promised her so to
do, which letters she caused to be read before him. And inas-
much as he had three wives living—first, herself ; then another in Scotland, of whom he had rid himself by purchase ;
last of all the Queen Mary—Mrs. Anna was of opinion that he
was not at all a person to be depended on ; he therefore promised her the yearly allowance of a hundred dollars from
Scotland, and gave her a pink, with an anchor, cable, and
other appurtenances."—*Marryat's Jutland,* chap. xxvii.

leaving, in a country not peculiarly temperate, records of hard drinking and wild carouses with those
who would join him in his revels. He died in the
Castle of Draxholm, and was buried in the church
of Farveile.[1] Not many years ago there came to
light a vindication of his conduct, written at some
length, and intended for a public state paper. It is
valuable only as showing the shape which the lies
of such a man put on. He maintained his own in-
nocence and that of the Queen, and both with
pretty equal success, showing how he was the un-
conscious victim of the machinations of Murray,
Lethington, and other his enemies. He left behind
him a shorter paper in the shape of a confession.
It is an example, added to countless others, of a
phenomenon peculiar to the nature of criminals—a
propensity to confess things not charged against
them, while denying those as to which guilt is
beyond possible question. With unseemly details,
the murderer of Darnley confesses to sins and vices
which nobody heard of and nobody cared about.
Among other things equally credible, he said he
owed his influence over Queen Mary to philters
and sweet waters."[2]

---

[1] Marryat's " Sweden," pp. 16-18.

[2] " Les affaires du Conte de Boduel," Bannatyne Club.
These papers will also be found among the " Documents
relatifs au meurtre de Darnley," printed by M. Teulet, in his
" Supplément au Recueil du Prince Labanoff," 1859.

[It may be mentioned that Jean, third daughter of George

fourth Earl of Huntly, the wife whom Bothwell divorced in order to effect his marriage with Mary Queen of Scots, afterwards, in 1573, married Alexander sixteenth Earl of Sutherland, ancestor, through this marriage of Elizabeth late Duchess Countess of Sutherland, mother of the Lady for whom this volume has been printed.—W. T.]

XVII.

I have suggested that the following extract should be made, and here inserted, from the Genealogical History of the Earldom of Sutherland, by Sir Robert Gordon, published in one volume, folio, Edinburgh, 1813, from a manuscript in the possession of Elizabeth Duchess Countess of Sutherland, then Marchioness of Stafford, and (in her own right) Countess of Sutherland, who is referred to in the preceding page. The extract relates (p. 146 of the work) a tragical history of the poisoning, in 1567, of John fifteenth Earl of Sutherland and his wife, the father and mother of Alexander the sixteenth Earl of Sutherland, referred to in the same note, and the narrow escape he had of being poisoned at the same time.—W. T.

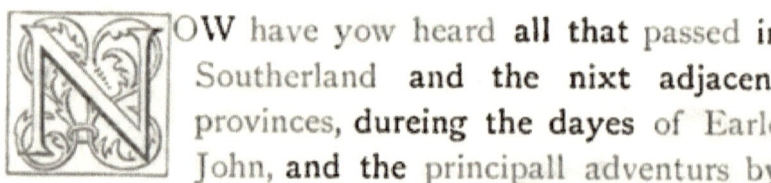

OW have yow heard all that passed in Southerland and the nixt adjacent provinces, dureing the dayes of Earle John, and the principall adventurs by armes which concerned these nighbouring cuntries whilest he lived; who, after he had passed his dayes, both at home in Scotland, and also abroad in other kingdomes, with great credet, and had bein divers tymes imployed in his prince's service, for the weill of his native cuntrey, he and his lady, who wes then big with chyld, were both together

poysoned at Helmisdale in Southerland, by Issobell
Sinclar (the wyff of Gilbert Gordoun of Gartay,
and the sister of William Sinclar, Laird of Dumbaith), at the instigation of George Sinclar, Earle
of Catteynes ; who after the death of Earle John,
took vpon him to punish the offenders ; doeing so
much the more in outward appearance, the lesse he
meant in heart, thinking by these meanes to frie himselff from the stain of such imputations. Yit the
Earle of Catteynes, by virtue of his pretended jus-
ticiarie within the bounds of the diocie of Catteynes,
did punish those who wer faithfullest to the Earle of
Southerland, and spaired the guyltie, who were
most suspected for that fact ; wherby he confirmed
in the hearts of all men the former opinion which
the world had of him touching the death of Earle
John.

" The Earle of Southerland's freinds perceaveing
how the Earle of Catteynes had indevoared to
shouffle over and cullor the matter, they appre-
hended Issobell Sinckler, and sent her to Edinburgh, to have her triall ther ; wher shoe died the
day of her execution, cursing alwise her cusin the
Earle of Catteynes, all the tyme of her seiknes,
evin untill the hour of her death.

" Alexander Gordoun, the onlie son of Earle
John, escaped verie narrowlie then from poysone ;
the same being also prepared and ordained for him,
which wes given to his father ; who, feilling himselff
past all hope of recovery, and perceaveing his sone

(as he came from hunting) making for supper, he took the table-cloath and threw it along the house, not suffering his sone to tast any meat or drink. So he, who wes then taking his last leave of the world, took also his last fareweill of his onlie sone ; and recommending him to the protection of God, and of his deirest freinds, he sent him the same night to Dounrobin, from Helmisdale, without his supper ; and from thence he wes conveyed to the castle of Skibo. Earle John and his Lady were caried the nixt morning to Dounrobin, wher both he and shoe, together with the chyld which wes in her bellie, died, all within fyve dayes after they were poysoned, in the moneth of Julie, the yeir of God 1567, and wer bureid in the cathedrall church at Dornogh.

"John Gordon, the eldest sone of Gilbert Gordoun of Gartay, and of this Issobell Sinclar, wes the nixt air-maill to the Earledome of Southerland, iff Earle John and his sone had both dyed, as wes intended ; with the which hope of succeiding to the earldome, this vainglorious woman wes led by her cousin, the Earle of Catteynes, and shoe did willinglie undertake, at his desyre, to execute this wicked villainy. Bot mark what then happened, and how God doth work in every thing according to his great and admirable providence. The sone of Issobell Sinckler (whom in her mynd and conceat shoe had appoynted to succeid) wes in the house with Earle John whil'st the poyson wes pre-

pairing, and the youth being thirstie, he called for
drink. One of her owne servants, who wes ignorant
of the practise, went in all hast, and brought vnto
the youth a drink of what shoe found readiest, being
a portion of the same wherin the poysone wes
mixed, which the youth drank, and died within tuo
dayes therefter : whose sudden death, and maner
therof, together with tokens which wer found and
remarked upon his bodie in the church of Golspie,
at his buriall, gave evin then a full assurance vnto
all men, that Issobell Sincler wes the author of
Earle Ihon his death ; shoe being also the fittest
instrument that the Earle of Catteynes, who hated
Earle Iohn mortallie, and repyned at his pros-
peritie, culd have vsed in the execution of this
tragedie ; serving his turne with that woman's cove-
tous ambitioun, and feiding her with a foolish hope,
that her sone should be Earle of Southerland, by
his meanes and assistance.

" Earle John, befor his going into Flanders, had
purchased from the bishop of Orknay the fue and
inheritance of the lands of Dounrey in Catteynes.
At his departure from Scotland, he gave the writs
and charters apperteyning to these lands in custodie
to William Sincler, Laird of Dumbaith, who had
mareid his sister Beatrix, and whom he maid his
tennent of these lands, thinking that he might
saiflie repose his trust and confidence in him. Bot
the Laird of Dumbaith, dureing Earle John his
banishment, took a new gift of these lands to his

owne use, and suppressed Earle John his writs.
Now, the Earle of Southerland being recalled, and
returning home, Dumbaith thought, that not onlie
wold Earle John endevoar to recover these lands,
bot also that all hope of pardon and reconciliatioun
with Earle John wes past. Wherevpon, joyning
with his cheiff and cousen, the Earle of Catteynes,
they vsed this ambitious woman (being Dumbaith
his sister) as a fitt instrument to execute this wicked
fact : which they beleivd shoe might easalie bring
to passe, being Gilbert Gordoun his wyff, and
duelling in Southerland. This is all I culd learn
concerning Earle John his death, and the authors
therof, whom God in his just judgement hath not
left vnpunished ; for Dumbaith his house and
familie is now perished, as wee sie, and his estate
is come into a stranger's hand. Ther is no lawfull
succession descended from the heyrs-maill of Gilbert Gordoun and Issobell Sinckler ; and shoe herselff died miserablie at Edinburgh, haveing (as wes
supposed) maid herselff away, least shoe should have
suffered a just punishment for so wicked a cryme ;
even at her last gasp still exclaiming against her
cousen, the Earle of Catteynes, and cursing him.
The Terrell of Doill his posteritie is decayed, and
run headlong to miserie, whos wyff was ane actrix
in this dolefull tragedie. Iohn, Master of Catteynes (the eldest sone of George Earle of Catteynes)
rose up and conspyred against his father, for the
which he imprissoned him in the Castle of Girnego,

wher he maid him die miserablie in wofull captivitie.
Earle George **his** second sone, William Sinckler,
wes slain by his owne brother John, who bruised
him to death in the castle of Girnego, **dureing his**
imprissonment **ther.** George **now Earle of Catteynes (grandchyld of olde Earle George), wes con-**
strained by the **authoritie of the** kingdome, **for**
divers crymes and **misdemeanors,** to forsak **his**
cuntrey and familie **a** long tyme. This **Earle**
George is at great jarrs and contentions **with his**
owne eldest sone, the **Lord Berridale, it being now**
almost hereditarie **to** this familie, that the father
and the sone should be at odds together. Besids
this, their house is over burdened and overwhelmed
with debts; wherby yow sie at this day the house
and earldome of Catteynes weill neir ane **vtter
rwyne,** liklie to vanish and fall **from the familie
and** surname of Sinckler. Thus is **the** Almightie
euer-liveing God a just revenger of innocent blood,
vpon the third and fourth generation. Happy ar
they who refer their vengeance **to** the Lord! **The**
onlie hope of that familie rests vpon the Lord
Berridale, his sone, a youth of singular good expectation.

XVIII.

REBELLION OF 1745.—FLORA MACDONALD.[1]

THE utmost diligence was used for seizing the Pretender's son; concerning whom there had been numberless reports; of which the following is the exactest, and seems most probable. On the 28th of June, he sailed in a small boat from South-Uist to the Isle of Sky, under the disguise of a young lady's maid. Next day they landed at a gentleman's house, having got a signal from a trusty friend on shore about half an hour before. Here the lady dined, with several others; but, though pressed to it, would not stay all night. After the lady and her pretended maid were gone hence, the Pretender's son resumed the habit of his sex, and was carried by John Macinnon, a boatman,

---

[1] Extracts from "The History of the Rebellion in 1745 and 1746, extracted from the "Scot's Magazine." 1 vol. 12mo. Aberdeen, 1755.

first to Raza, and then back to Sky, and at last to
the Continent." After describing his subsequent
movements in this page 247 and the next, it goes
on to say, "He was at that time" (20 July) "reported to be wandering about in Morar, in an old
highland habit, and in a bad state of health, being
broke out to such a degree, that he was like a
leper."

In a subsequent part of the book, at p. 273, &c.,
a more full account is given. After stating various
movements of the young man and his attendants,
it goes on thus: "At night they sailed for Loch-
busdale; where they arrived, and staid eight days on
a rock, making a tent of the sail of the boat. They
found themselves then in a most dreadful situa-
tion; for having intelligence that Captain Scott
had landed at Kylbride, the company was obliged
to separate; and the Pretender and O'Neil went to
the mountains; where they remained all night, and
soon after were informed that General Campbell
was at Bernera; so that now they had forces very
near, on both sides of them, and were absolutely at
a loss which way to move. In their road they met
with a young lady, one Miss Macdonald, to whom
Captain O'Neil proposed assisting the Pretender to
make his escape; which she at first refused; but
on his promising to put on woman's clothes she
consented, and desired them to go to the mountain
of Currada, till she sent for them; where they accordingly staid two days; but hearing nothing from
the young lady, the Pretender concluded she

would not keep her word, and therefore resolved to send Captain O'Neil to General Campbell, to let **him** know he was willing to surrender to him. **But** about five in the evening, a message came from the young lady desiring them to meet her **at** Rushness. Being afraid to pass by the ford, because of the militia, they luckily found a boat which carried them over **to the** other side of Uia, where they remained part of the day, afraid of being seen by the country people. In the evening they set out for Rushness, and arrived there at twelve at night; **but** not finding the young lady, and being alarmed by **a** boat-full of militia, they were obliged to retire two miles back; where **the** Pretender remained on **a** moor, till O'Neil went to the young lady, and prevailed upon her to come to the place appointed at nightfall or next day. About an hour after they had account of General Campbell's arrival at Benbicula, which obliged them to remove to another part of the island; whence, as the day broke, they discovered four sail close on the shore, making directly up to the place where they were; so that there was nothing left for them to do, but to throw themselves among the heath. When the wherries were gone, they resolved to go to Clanronald's house. But when they were within a mile of it, they heard that General Campbell was there, which forced them to retreat again; and soon after O'Neil was taken. The young Pretender having at length, with the assistance of Captain O'Neil, found Miss Macdonald in **a cottage** near the place appointed,

it was there determined, that he should put on
women's clothes and pass for her waiting maid.
This being done he took leave of Sullivan and
O'Neil with great regret; who departed to shift
for themselves, leaving him and his new mistress
in the cottage; where they continued some days,
during which she cured him of the itch. Upon intelligence that General Campbell was gone further
into the country, they removed to her cousin's; and
spent the night in preparing for their departure to
the Isle of Sky. Accordingly they set out the next
morning, with only one man servant, named Maclean, and two rowers. During their voyage they
were pursued by a small vessel; but, a thick fog
rising, they arrived safe at midnight in that island,
and landed at the foot of a rock, where the lady
and maid waited, while her man Maclean went to
see if Sir Alexander Macdonald was at home.
Maclean found his way thither, but lost it returning back. His mistress and her maid, after in vain
expecting him the whole night, were obliged in the
morning to leave the rock, and go in the boat up
the creek to some distance, to avoid the militia
which guarded the coast. They went on shore again
about ten o'clock, and attended by the rowers, in-
quired the way to Sir Alexander's. When they
had gone about two miles, they met Maclean: he
told his lady that Sir Alexander was with the
Duke of Cumberland; but his lady was at home,
and would do them all the service she could.

Whereupon they discharged their boat, and went directly to the house ; where they remained two days ; Betty living always in her lady's chamber, except o' night, to prevent a discovery. But a party of the Macleods, having intelligence that some strangers were arrived at Sir Alexander's, and knowing his lady was well affected to the Pretender, came thither, and demanding to see the new-comers, were introduced to Miss's chamber, where she sat with her new maid. The latter hearing the militia was at the door, had the presence of mind to get up and open it ; which occasioned his being less taken notice of ; and after they had narrowly searched the closets they withdrew. The inquiry however alarmed the lady, and the next day she sent her maid to a steward of Sir Alexander's, Macdonald of Kinsburgh, ten miles distant ; where he remained but one day, for on receiving intelligence that it was rumoured he was disguised in a woman's habit, Kingsburgh furnished him with a suit of his own clothes, and he went in a boat to Macleod of Raza's."—Other wanderings are then mentioned, in one of which it is said "he went over the hill of Morar in a tattered highland habit."

From these accounts, it would appear that Miss Macdonald took charge of the fugitive unwillingly, and that she got rid of him as soon as she could. It would also appear that her success in curing him of the itch was not altogether effectual, as when afterwards in Morar he was "like a leper." —W. T.

I

XIX.

FATAL BANDITTI ADVENTURE IN ASIA MINOR.[1]

Rhodes, Nov. 29, 1845.

 HAVE written to Colonel Jones, Ord-
nance Storekeeper at Chatham, telling
him of the sad and sudden death of my
companion and his nephew, Sir Lawrence Jones—for in Lady Jones's (the mother's)
state of health, I was afraid of writing directly to
her at Cheltenham. In case of his absence or re-
moval from Chatham, &c. will you have the goodness to enquire for the letter at Chatham, and if
necessary cause it to be sent immediately to him, or
to another uncle at Woolwich (Colonel Jones also).
For this will get into the Constantinople papers,
and be perhaps transferred to the English, &c.
We had nearly finished our tour, and we were on
our way to Smyrna, eight hours past Macri (a small
port opposite Rhodes), when we were suddenly

---

[1] Letter from Captain Richard Twopeny (formerly of the
52nd Regiment) to his brother, Edward Twopeny, Esq. of
Woodstock, in Kent.

attacked by an ambush of Xebecs (disbanded Ja-
nissaries, notorious robbers). Poor Jones and the
servant were shot dead on the spot, and I was
wounded, but am now nearly well, and hope to sail
for Smyrna to-morrow.

On the morning of the 7th November we broke
up our encampment early (having slept in the tent
four hours from Macri) and started for Dollomon, on
the way to Smyrna—track very mountainous and
bad—the day beautiful. Our party consisted of,—
first, a Turk, owner of the horses : he is an Imaüm
(priest) from Xanthus, mounted and armed with a
musket and a girdle of cartridges ; then a Greek
man and a lad from Macri, on foot, unarmed and
driving two baggage-horses ; then a Smyrniote Greek
servant, mounted, unarmed ; then Sir L. Jones
mounted, a brace of pistols in holsters ; last, myself,
mounted, unarmed. We always travelled in file, from
the badness of the tracks. About mid-day the
Imaüm suddenly stopped, and began to fix his flint,
prime, &c. Both he and the servant had seen some
Xebecs skulking about and endeavouring to hide
among the bushes ahead. Jones happened to be
behind for a moment. When he came up I said, not
thinking much of it at the moment—" Prepare for a
general action." It was a little valley full of high
bushes, and opening out upon the sea. He went to
the end of it, the Imaüm at the "ready." No
Xebecs. Here the road began to ascend a ravine,
and was thickly hemmed in with bushes for many

hundred yards on each side. We momentarily
expected an attack. In a quarter of an hour we
came to a fountain surrounded by oak trees, under-
neath free of bushes. Said Jones, "We may as
well stop to lunch here. If these fellows mean to
attack us, we can't escape them ; and it is better
to fight on a full stomach than an empty one."
" Perhaps," said I, "our numbers looked formidable,
and they hardly know how slightly armed we are."
" I can hardly think so little of Turkish courage,"
he replied. In my own mind, I felt that they were
probably skulking alongside among the bushes, and
that stopping was imprudent, as it gave them plenty
of time to head us and choose their ground. But
as he seemed bent on it I did not oppose him. We
were about twenty minutes at luncheon, discussing
the merits of the things put before us just as usual.
The Greek lad's horse was a slow one, so he was
sent ahead when we first sat down to eat. After
luncheon we had not proceeded more than ten
minutes up the hill, when on passing a large mass
of rock about eight feet high, and which abutted on
the road on our right, a volley of musketry burst
on us from behind it, distance about three yards.
At the same instant poor Jones and the servant fell
heavily from their horses, and I received a ball in
my left breast, and instantly after another, as I
thought, in my right, and various slug wounds. My
little pony contrived to wriggle himself from under
me and disappeared, and I found myself standing

in the middle of the road. At this moment Jones's
horse, just disengaged from his rider, came gallop-
ing down past me. I seized the bridle, took the
pistols out of the holsters, and let him go. As I
turned round I saw poor Jones and the servant in
their last struggles. I looked up at the rock to see
if I could make anything of a fight. Slightly mys-
tified by the blue smoke of the firing and some
straggling branches, I distinguished the tops of five
or six turbaned heads looking along their musket-
barrels, which rested on the top of the rock and
were pointed at me. Reflecting **that** they **were six**
to one—that they were so well covered that they
left me nothing to aim at—that I was without am-
munition to reload, and that I was entirely exposed
to them, and every moment becoming fainter from
loss of blood, I settled instantly that resistance
would be madness, so threw down my pistols, and sunk
down weak and giddy beside them. They instantly
rushed out of their hiding-place, took up the pistols
and surrounded me, shouting "Paras, paras!" (a small
Turkish coin). I handed them the trifle I had about
me and my watch. "Paras!" again they cried.
I pointed up towards the luggage, and they immediately set to work to rifle it, obliging the Greek
man and the Imaüm (deprived of his musket) to
assist them. I remained quiet. Just above me were
the dead bodies of poor Jones and the servant, and
just above them the robbers, luggage, &c. Presently
the Imaüm came running down past me, and I sup-

posed that they had suffered him to escape, so I
thought I might as well try, so I got up staggering,
and as I fell again from weakness, I saw that some
of them had left off their ransacking to level their
muskets at me. Presently the Imaüm returned; he
had only been sent, I fancy, to see if the coast was
clear. I remained quiet. The robbers were perhaps
two hours hunting for money. They then marched
down in file, in regular military style, between the
dead bodies and past me, followed by a young
man who seemed to be their captain. They were
six in all, armed each with a musket and a girdle
of cartridges, in which was stuck a brace of large
pistols and a sword. As the Captain was passing
me, he stopped for a moment and said " Paras." I
again pointed to the baggage. At this moment
one of the band stepped out of his rank, turned
round, and deliberately took aim at me. I was
momentarily expecting the ball to crash through
me, when the Captain waved the musket up with
his hand, and they marched away. I crawled up
to poor Jones, and found him quite dead. Just
above, the Imaüm and the Greek were arranging
the fragments of our baggage on three horses. I
made signs to them to put Jones's body on one of
them ; this they positively refused to do again and
again, drawing their fingers across their throats,
and saying, " Xebec." The Interpreter being dead,
I was obliged to give in. However, I got the
Imaüm to turn the body on its back, and take off a

ring and cut off some of his hair for his mother. We also found some money in his pockets—for some superstitious scruple, the robbers had hardly touched the bodies. The Imaüm then lifted me upon one of the horses. The constrained position of the Turkish saddle made me almost faint away, whereupon they put me on another, which had a great pile of horsecloths, and no stirrups, &c. and we started for Macri. It wanted an hour of sunset. I found the sun very hot on my back—I was hot, bleeding, faint, and parched. We crossed some streams, and I drank like a fish. Soon the sun went down, and a fresh east breeze sprung up, which refreshed me. A bright moon came to our aid, without which we could never have kept such a difficult mountain track. Down hill the jolting of the horse was agonizing, and without stirrups, and my legs over his shoulders, I was perpetually in danger of slipping over his head, and the hills were numerous and excessively steep. I wanted to stop and rest, for I despaired of ever reaching Macri, but the Imaüm would not hear of it, and said, "Xebec, Xebec." So at midnight, almost done, and bleeding profusely, I arrived there—eight hours on the road. We knocked up the only European, Mr. Biliotti, the Tuscan Consul (whose acquaintance I had made two days before). When the worthy man was sufficiently awake to take it all in, he received me with all the affectionate *warmth of a near relation.* Nothing could exceed his kindness; and the sight and the story made him quite ill. Before daylight we dispatched a boat for the bodies, with the Imaüm as a guide. Then a French renegade Turk, who had a smattering of surgery, stopped the bleeding and bandaged my wounds. In the afternoon, the boat returned with the bodies. I was too weak to move. So Mr. Biliotti kindly superintended their interment in the Court of the Greek Church. I was then carried down and put on board a boat for Rhodes, for the sake of proper medical advice. I arrived safely next morning. Mr. Wilkinson, the English Consul, received me most kindly, got a room and a servant, &c. A little German Dr. (Dr. Barman) examined my wounds. The ball in my left breast, just over my heart, had come side ways, glanced off the breast bone, and gone out at the nipple, making a tunnel of about two inches—tedious to cure, but of no consequence. The other was a volley of slugs, one of which hit a vein in the breast, and I fancied was a ball. They hit me six times in the head and face, and seven times in the body. They have given a little trouble, but are of no consequence. I have been three weeks in bed, and am very weak; but I am now up and preparing for my voyage with the appetite of a horse. I hope to be in time for the 10. Malta steamer, where I shall have eight days quarantine, and go on to Naples for Rome by next steamer, which leaves Smyrna on the 20th, or I may find a Trieste or Ancona one. People cannot make out why the Xebecs spared me. Perhaps they thought that I should be left there and must die, and therefore a charge of powder was waste. It is considered almost miraculous, and I can only attribute it to the mercy of Almighty God. Take care not to frighten my good mother. I have made the Imaüm a present, for he is a real good fellow, and saved my life.

Copy of part of a later Letter from Rome.

Rome, 31 January, 1846.

You kindly enquire after my wounds. One slug went down to the bone, on the right and upper side of the head, a little above the commencement of the hair. It took some time to heal, and the doctor could not find the lead. I believe that it is there still, as there is a lump near it, but it does no harm. A little more or less lead in one's head makes no difference. Next, the bone of the cavity of the eye near the outside of the right eye-brow arrested another slug, which otherwise would certainly have put my eye out. One grazed my ear, another my nose, and two buried themselves in the lower jaw just within the whisker. These I have ; they were extracted with some little pain. None of them have left disfiguring marks. Those on my body have left small damask marks, but they are of no manner of consequence, any of them. The bullet wound is entirely healed, and has, of course, left a considerable scar. The ladies rather bully me for not looking pale and interesting, and every body tells me that I never looked so fresh or so fat. I am, of course, a nine days' wonder.

[Good was derived from the evil of this tragical adventure. Owing to the strong representations of the English Ambassador then at Constantinople, Sir Stratford Canning, now Viscount Stratford de Redcliffe, the Turkish Government for the first time exerted itself in endeavours, which were ultimately successful, to capture these lawless Banditti. In doing so, one, (the captain as was supposed,) was killed. A difficulty arose as to trying the survivors for their offence, there being only one Mahomedan witness; their law requiring in such a case two, both Mahomedans, the evidence of the Christians not being received. The Turkish Government offered to confine the culprits for life without trial. Sir Stratford Canning refused to accept that as a satisfaction, and required that the law as to not receiving the evidence of Christians should be altered. Ultimately a Court was established, in which in future the evidence of Christians would be received.

Ten days before the receipt of this letter, an account appeared in the newspapers from Constantinople, shortly stating the murder of Sir Lawrence Jones, and that my brother had been wounded, but giving no particulars of what had become of him. During the period of this painful suspense, my mother, to whom my brother refers, showed, by her patient submission, what can be effected by Christian resignation.

The letter, from the extreme weakness of the writer, occupied him several days ; but it has no evidence, either from its style or otherwise, of having been written at broken intervals.—W. T.]

PRINTED BY WHITTINGHAM AND WILKINS,
TOOKS COURT, CHANCERY LANE.